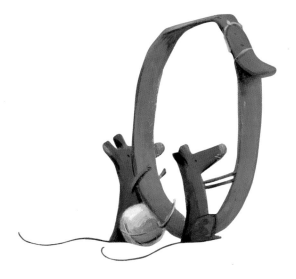

BELLING the TIGER

BELLING the TIGER

by Mary Stolz

Illustrated by Pierre Pratt

Running Press
KIDS
PHILADELPHIA·LONDON

Library of Congress Control Number: 2003115604
ISBN 0-7624-1889-3

Designed by Frances J. Soo Ping Chow
Acquired by Patty Aitken Smith
Edited by Patty Aitken Smith and Susan K. Hom
Typography: Elroy and Bodoni

This book may be ordered by mail from the publisher.
Please include $2.50 for postage and handling.
But try your bookstore first!

Published by Running Press Kids,
an imprint of Running Press Book Publishers
125 South Twenty-second Street
Philadelphia, Pennsylvania 19103-4399

Visit us on the web!
www.runningpress.com

IN A SEASIDE TOWN, in a house by the docks, the mice met in a closet and decided to bell the cat. Ever since time and cats and mice began, mice have been meeting in closets, telling each other what a good idea this would be. You get a collar with a bell, you hang it around the cat's neck, and ever after that you hear her coming.

"What a sensible notion," said a pantry mouse to a living-room mouse. "Why hasn't anyone thought of it before?"

"I think someone has," said the living-room mouse, who had the run of the library, but no one listened to him.

"The meeting will come to order," said their leader, a kitchen mouse named Portman. He was silver, going gray, and knew what there was to know, from cellar to attic. He was an extremely fierce mouse, and all the others obeyed him without question.

Now he looked around at the meeting, which was small because the cat they were discussing was large, and said, "Friends, the time has come when we can no longer allow this July, this *cat*, to go about free as air and quiet as a wink. He is reducing our ranks and making life miserable for all of us."

"True, true," said the meeting, as one mouse.

"Therefore," said Portman in a deep squeak, "your Steering Committee has come up with a solution."

"What's a Steering Committee?" said Bob, one of the two smallest mice, to his brother, Ozzie, the other smallest mouse.

"It's Portman and his friends deciding before the meeting starts what we're going to decide in the meeting," said Ozzie.

"Is that fair?" said Bob.

"It's customary," said Ozzie.

"I see," said Bob.

If there was one thing he'd learned in his short life, it was that what was customary could not be argued with. Custom saw to it that smaller mice were kept in their place, held their tongues, got the ragtag ends of provender and treats, got assigned to places where they'd rather not be. He and Ozzie were cellar mice, and Bob didn't like it down there. It was damp, and there wasn't enough light.

"NOW," SAID PORTMAN SOLEMNLY, "your Steering Committee has decided that July must be belled without further delay. We are met here to decide who among us is to be chosen for this honor."

"We are too small," Ozzie said in his brother's ear, "to be concerned in such large doings. Let's not listen."

They squinched close together, and together they were not as big as Portman.

The big mice talked for quite a while, saying the same thing over in different ways so as to make it a proper meeting, and then they announced that the time had come to elect the bell mouse, the hero.

"The way we'll do it," said Portman, "is this. When I say *Decide!*, everyone is to look at somebody. The mouse at whom most of us look will be our elected hero."

It was understood that Portman, as leader, was not to be looked at.

"Decide!" yelled Portman.

Nobody wanted to create any hard feelings, so all the big mice avoided looking at one another. In the end, they turned to the back of the hall and looked at the two smallest mice, who made the mistake of looking at each other.

"A just and unanimous decision," said Portman. "Let the two heroes come to the front of the hall."

Bob and Ozzie inched forward.

"We're too young to be heroes," said Ozzie nervously when they were standing in front of Portman. His sharp eyes frightened them, and they curled their tails together for comfort.

"Nonsense," said Portman. "It's always the youngest son who gets chosen for the adventure. That's customary. If the youngest son happens to be twins . . . well, that's two of them. Meeting dispersed."

IN A TWINKLING THE CLOSET WAS EMPTY of all but the two smallest mice, who crowded nose to nose and stared into each other's eyes.

"They mean us," said Ozzie. "We get to be the heroes."

"I guess so," said Bob, looking around. "Everybody else is gone. How do you suppose we start?"

Ozzie said he didn't know. "Where's the cat?" he asked.

"Where's the collar?" said Bob.

Of the two, it would be easier to find the cat, so they decided to look for a collar. There was no such thing in the house, and they would have to go out to the shops by the waterfront to see if a collar with a bell on it was to be found there.

They slid through a crack in the baseboard into the garden, then ran along cobbled streets, keeping close to the house fronts. They moved as if they had little wheels to run on past the grocer's, the tailor's, the fishmonger's, the baker's, and at length they came to the hardware store.

There, on a rack high above their heads, next to some harnesses and leashes, was an assortment of collars with bells on. *For Kitty*, said a sign above the rack.

"We've come to the right place," said Bob. "Only how will we get up there?"

The two mice, small and shining, tipped their heads up, curled their tails, and studied the distance.

"Well," said Ozzie when they'd looked quite a while, "one of us must climb up there and knock a collar off the rack and hurry down again, and then the two of us must pick it up and run as fast as we can back to the house."

"What do we do then?" said Bob uneasily.

"Rest," said Ozzie, who was already tired from being a hero.

They sat in the shadow of a wheelbarrow and considered the problem. There was a pile of boxes that would probably be easy enough to climb, but it would require a fearful jump if one of them was to reach the rack where the collars were. Neither one of them wanted to try the jump, and neither wanted the other to try it either.

They stared upward, and the longer they stared, the higher the collars seemed and the farther the jump from the boxes to the rack.

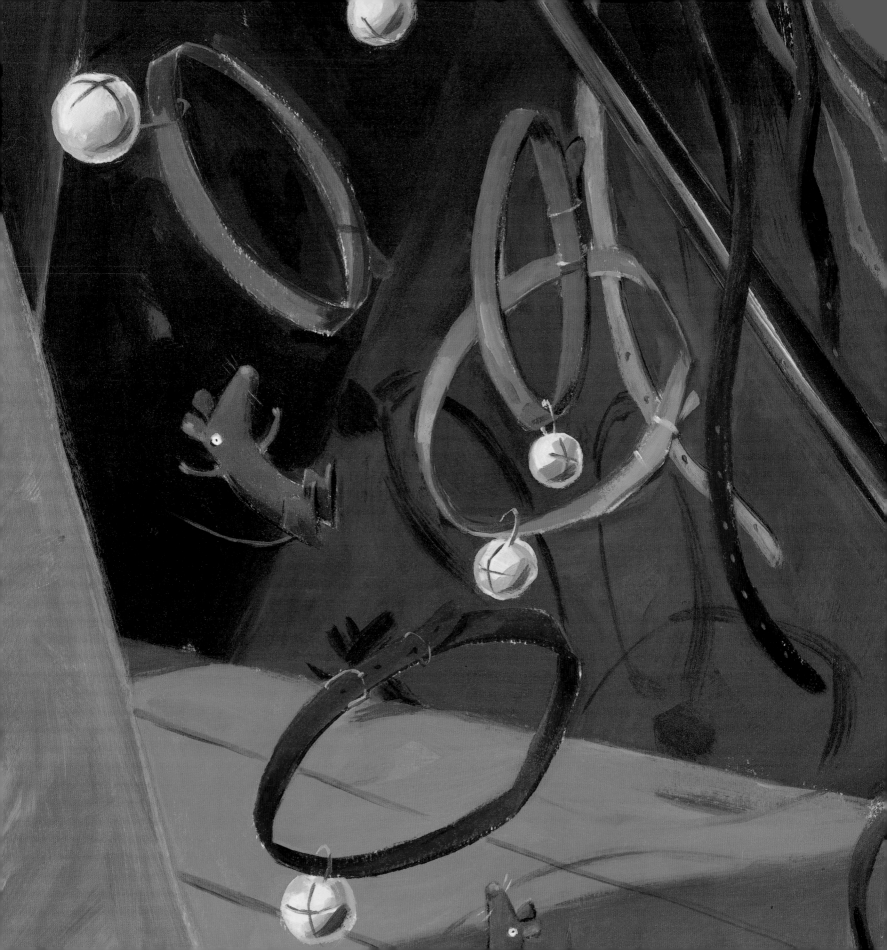

"LET'S GO HOME and say we couldn't find any," said Bob at length. But Ozzie didn't answer. Because they both knew that they were more afraid of Portman than they were of the long jump, or even of July the cat. After all, they might manage the jump, and July never came down in the cellar, but Portman was with them always—big and cross and the boss of everything.

"Well," said Ozzie suddenly, "here goes."

Before Bob could say a word, Ozzie had whisked up the boxes. When he reached the top he didn't take time to think or to judge the distance—he just flew through the air and the rack and landed, tottering and off balance, on top of the collars. Gently the rack swayed, tilted. The collars began to slide off, and down came Ozzie in a jingle of bells and leather, right beside his brother, Bob.

"Are you hurt?" Bob squeaked.

"We'll find out later," said Ozzie, and the two of them seized a bright blue collar in their tiny sharp teeth and began to run as the hardware man appeared jumping up and down in his doorway. The collar tipped backward, and they had to lift their heads to keep it from encircling them altogether. They ran desperately, holding the collar like a hoop, unable to see where they were going.

Suddenly they heard a soft sound of pleasure directly behind them, a sound that could mean only one thing. A cat had spied them. Redoubling their efforts, they ran blindly, losing all sense of direction. Down the cobbled streets they flew and across the docks, swift as quicksilver, with the cat racing behind them. Not for a moment did they think of dropping the collar. It was their achievement, the first they'd made in the world, and they would not let it go. Holding it up, they fled down the docks, up a great rope, and onto the deck of a ship.

THERE THEY STOPPED and sat in the circle of the collar, their tails looped over each other's backs, and stared down at the dock, where a big cat looked up at them with glinting eyes. Lazily, as if he had all the time in the world, the cat began to saunter toward the gangplank.

"Now what?" said Bob. "Down the rope again?"

"He'd just turn around and be on us like a . . . like a cat," said Ozzie.

"But if we stay here, he'll have the whole ship to hunt us down in."

Just then a man on deck yelled, "Take 'er away!" and before that big self-confident cat had time to reach it, the gangplank had been wheeled onto the dock and a deafening bellow from the ship's funnel announced that she was ready to sail.

Bob and Ozzie peeped over to jeer at the cat. He pretended not to see them. He pretended he hadn't really wanted to walk up that gangplank at all. He pretended to wash his paws.

"They're awfully proud," said Bob.

"Yes," said Ozzie. "Cats are known for their pride."

They sat within the circle of the blue collar, looking down at the proud cat getting smaller and smaller as the ship left the dock behind.

"It looks as if we're going to sea," said Ozzie after a while.

"Portman isn't going to like it," said Bob.

They hunched together nervously. Portman would bristle and snap and his eyes would flash, and the longer they delayed the more all this would happen, and it was too awful to think of.

So they decided not to think of it.

THEY HAD TO FIND A PLACE to store their collar, and then a place to live, and then they had to see about eating arrangements, and one way and another whole days and nights went by during which they didn't give home and Portman a thought.

"What we have to decide," said Ozzie one night as they munched dreamily on a bun that had rolled into a corner of the ship's galley, "is what to do when the boat docks. I mean, here we are, having a sea voyage, and July can't be belled till we get back. On the other hand, when will we ever take a trip again? It would be a pity not to see something of another land while we have the chance."

"Portman won't like it," said Bob.

"Somehow," said Ozzie thoughtfully, "that doesn't sound very scary now, does it?"

"No," said Bob. "Of course," he pointed out, "it may sound scary when we get back home again."

Ozzie finished up a raisin and smoothed his whiskers. "Let's worry about that when we get home," he said.

The night the ship tied up they slipped down the rope to see a new land. Someone might have heard the tinkle of a bell as they carried their collar like a hoop above their heads, but no one paid any attention, and they made their way into the darkness undisturbed.

A new land, and a strange one. A land of thick twining vines, huge pulpy leaves, and ropy grass. A land of mystifying sounds. Cackles and roars and whistles and slitherings in the gloom.

When they'd walked a long way, they stopped to rest beside a plant that looked like a great green trumpet folding toward the ground.

"It's a lot noisier in this country at night than it is at home," said Bob.

"I wonder what those roaring sounds are," Ozzie mused. He sniffed the air and turned his head from side to side. "You know, Bob, I get the funniest feeling of *cat* about this place. Not cat like July, but still . . . cat. Do you know what I mean?"

Bob nodded. He was uneasy, but did not like to show it for fear of upsetting his brother. He wanted one of them to be brave, and figured it had better be Ozzie. But there was a *cat* feeling about this place. Bigger than a July feeling, but the same, somehow.

"Maybe we should go back to the ship," he said.

"Where is it?" said Ozzie.

They didn't know.

"Well," said Ozzie, sounding brave, "maybe we'd better go to sleep."

So they dragged the collar under the tremendous protecting leaves of the trumpet plant and looped their tails together and went to sleep.

17

AT DAWN they woke to a hot curling mist that dripped heavily off vines and leaves. The air was still full of shrieks and snarls and caws, and the moist undergrowth seemed alive with sly movements.

Bob and Ozzie peered out from between the folds of the trumpet plant and longed for their quiet cellar at home. "What's this?" said Ozzie. He was looking at a black-and-gold thing quite close to them. It was furred. It breathed. It was so big that Ozzie wondered if at last he was seeing a mountain.

"I don't think mountains breathe," said Bob as they crept out from beneath the trumpet plant. He peered at a large object near his nose. Suddenly his whiskers trembled. "This is a *paw*," he whispered.

"Paw?" said Ozzie. "What paw?"

"How should I know what paw?" said Bob, very excited. "But come see for yourself. It's a paw, and it looks like a cat's paw." He tipped his head way back, till he almost fell over, but the slopes of the black-and-gold stripes seemed to reach to the sky.

Ozzie came over and studied the paw. He had to agree that in everything but size it could have been

July's. "But how can that be a cat?" he demanded. "They couldn't get it in the house."

"Let's walk around it," said Bob.

They took a trip around this thing they had found, and from every angle, even viewed from above—when they climbed some vines to get a better look—it looked like a cat. It was bigger than a hundred Julys, maybe two hundred Julys, but something about it said *cat*.

"Are you afraid?" said Bob.

"I don't think so. I mean, I'm not as afraid of this as I am of July," said Ozzie.

"Or Portman."

"Or Portman," Ozzie agreed. "This thing is so big. We could be under something before it saw us."

"Whoever would think a cat could get so big," said Bob in awe.

"Maybe we'd better go away," said Ozzie. "I think we've seen enough of a foreign land, don't you?"

"No," said Bob, and clutched his brother. "No. I have an idea."

NOW SINCE THEY'D BEEN BORN, Ozzie had always been the one to have ideas. This was Bob's very first. So even though he wanted very much to find the ship and go home, Ozzie waited to see what Bob's idea would be.

"Let us," said Bob thrillingly, "bell this cat."

They looked at each other for a long time, and then both heads turned toward the tremendous sleeper.

"It's a cat," Bob insisted. "It's the biggest cat anyone has ever seen. Think if *we* should be the ones to bell it."

Ozzie, now filled with excitement, looked at the blue collar. His head drooped. "Oh Bob. How silly you are. This collar wouldn't even go around his nose."

"It will go around his *tail!*" said Bob triumphantly.

They began to run around in a frenzy of pleasure. For it would, it would, the blue collar would go nicely around the end of the giant cat's tail, and they would be mouse heroes. Who cared about belling July when you could bell a cat like this?

"Portman will care," Ozzie said.

They grew quiet, and sat down to think it over. Yes, Portman would care very much indeed, and would be indeed very angry. They thought about this, and they looked at the black-and-gold breathing mountain, especially at its twitching tail, and suddenly Bob said, "Who cares about Portman?"

For a moment Ozzie looked astonished, and then he jumped up saying, "Who cares, who cares, who cares *what* Portman thinks . . .?" and carefully they dragged the collar to the end of the gently stirring tail.

"Now, look," said Ozzie. "We'll hold the collar up, and the next time the tail twitches . . . woosh! and we'll have it on."

Bob nodded happily. They lifted the collar in their paws and held it, waiting. One twitch . . . They leaned forward . . . no, too late. They waited again. Another twitch . . . too late again . . . A wait, and then another twitch . . . Forward they leaned . . . and *there!* The collar was around the black thick fur of the great tail . . . and . . .

What happened then they did not expect.

They had not had time to release the collar when the tail went high in the air, and there they hung, kicking and squeaking wildly, while the bell tinkled and the tail thrashed and the world reeled around. Bob, who was getting very daring, had a moment to think what a glorious way to die, but Ozzie only wished they'd stayed on the boat.

They hung and swung, and gradually the motion of the tail gentled, and the biggest cat face they'd ever seen turned and studied them. Bob and Ozzie closed their eyes. The sight was too fearsome.

"AND WHAT'S ALL THIS?" said a deep, dark voice. "What's this that's got attached to my tail?"

Bob and Ozzie didn't answer.

"Speak up!" said the voice more sternly, and the two mice realized it hadn't sounded too cross when it first spoke.

"It's us," said the mice quickly. "Ozzie and Bob."

"Ozzie and Bob, eh? Well, Ozzie and Bob, open your eyes."

Fearfully, slowly, they opened their eyes and most courageously did not close them again.

"What are you doing there?" said the great cat.

"Hanging on," squeaked Ozzie.

"Comfy?" asked the cat.

They shook their heads.

With great care the cat swung his tail over, lowering it so they could step onto his flanks. The motion of his breath was like the motion of the ship, and they had to steady themselves by gripping his fur.

Summoning all his courage, Bob said, "What . . . I mean, are you a cat?"

The big creature nodded, and Bob and Ozzie, who'd been hoping it would not be true, trembled and hung on. They were sitting on the side of a cat and talking to it, and there was no way to get down, and they decided this was the end of them.

"In a manner of speaking," the cat went on. "I'm a tiger, really."

"That's what July is," Ozzie said faintly. "A tiger cat."

"Who's July?"

"The cat that lives in our house," said Bob.

"Lives in the house?" said the tiger. "Ridiculous."

"Oh, no. July has lived in the house forever. She's only about as big as your paw."

"A cub," said the tiger. "A baby. Small, though, even for a baby."

"July's not a baby," said Ozzie. "She's eight years old."

"And as big as my paw?" The tiger thought it over. "Remarkable. What sort of country do you come from?"

Ozzie and Bob didn't know. It was the country they came from, but they did not know how to say what sort it was, except that cats there never got too big to fit in the houses.

"Why are you trembling so?" the tiger asked with interest. "The two of you are jostling my fur something awful."

"We're afraid—" Bob began, and Ozzie pinched him, but it was too late and he'd already finished "—you'll eat us."

"Eat you?" the tiger roared. "Why, I'd as soon eat a . . . a mouse!"

The two brothers fell into each other's arms and prepared to die.

"Now what's the matter?" said the tiger.

"But we are mice," Ozzie quaked.

THE TIGER STUDIED THEM with even greater interest. "Are you, now? You know, I've never seen a mouse before. I've heard of them, of course. They scare elephants. But I've never seen one. That was just a manner of speaking. Like saying I'd as soon eat a coconut. Have you ever seen a coconut?"

"No," they said, hoping they never would, if a coconut was anything like a tiger.

"What's an elephant?" Ozzie asked, thinking that, whatever it was, it must be pretty small and nervous to be frightened by a mouse.

"Oh, he's a huge loud fellow with great ears and a trunk. Nothing bigger in the jungle, truth to tell. Not that size is everything." The tiger looked at his little visitors and said, "You don't appear to believe me."

"Well," said Ozzie, "it isn't that, exactly. But the biggest creature in the jungle being scared by us? It isn't *easy* to believe."

"Hmm," said the tiger. He pricked up his ears, listened to the air for a moment, and said, "Climb to the top of my back. I'm going to stand up. There, now," he went on, when he was on his feet and the two mice were clinging to his backbone. "You see this great animal bearing down on us?"

The two mice looked, blinked, looked again. Then they sank into the tiger's fur as though hiding in grass. Along a narrow path came a tremendous, gray, flap-eared, hose-nosed, thunder-footed creature that surely was bigger than a living thing had a right to be.

"Good-bye, Bob," said Ozzie.

"Good-bye," Bob whispered.

"Ho, there, Elephant!" the tiger called.

The elephant came to a lordly halt, glanced over at the tiger, and said, "Well?"

"Come see what I have on my back," the tiger invited slyly.

"Why?"

"I'm trying to prove a point to some friends of mine."

The elephant came forward suspiciously. "Where are your friends?"

"Here on my back," said the tiger. "See!"

The elephant leaned over, spied the two mice cringing in the tiger's fur, and with one great trumpet that shivered the trees around them, turned and fled down the path, waving his trunk wildly.

"WHAT DID I TELL YOU?" said the tiger when the crashing and bellowing had died in the distance. "He's simply terrified of mice. But a brave fellow, for all that. It's nothing to be ashamed of . . . a fear or two. Most of us have them. Not me, of course," he said modestly. "But then . . . I *am* a tiger."

Bob and Ozzie were overcome with what they had just seen. A beast as big as a building fleeing from the mere sight of them.

"Will they ever believe us at home when we tell them?" said Bob.

"Will we ever be home to tell them at all?" said Ozzie.

The tiger began to wave his tail about gracefully, admiring his blue collar, and the mice clung desperately, calling out, "Tiger! Be careful!"

"Oh . . . am I disturbing you? Sorry. It's just that I admire this pretty present so much. Don't you think the blue looks well on me?"

"Very becoming," said Bob and Ozzie together.

The tiger thanked them formally for the gift.

"And now," he said, "what can I do for you in return?"

The mice eyed each other with rising hope.

"Could you," said Ozzie, "take us back to the ship, so we could go home?"

The tiger thought it over. "I can't take you right to the ship," he said at length. "It would cause a commotion. But I can take you close enough and direct you from there. Would that suit?"

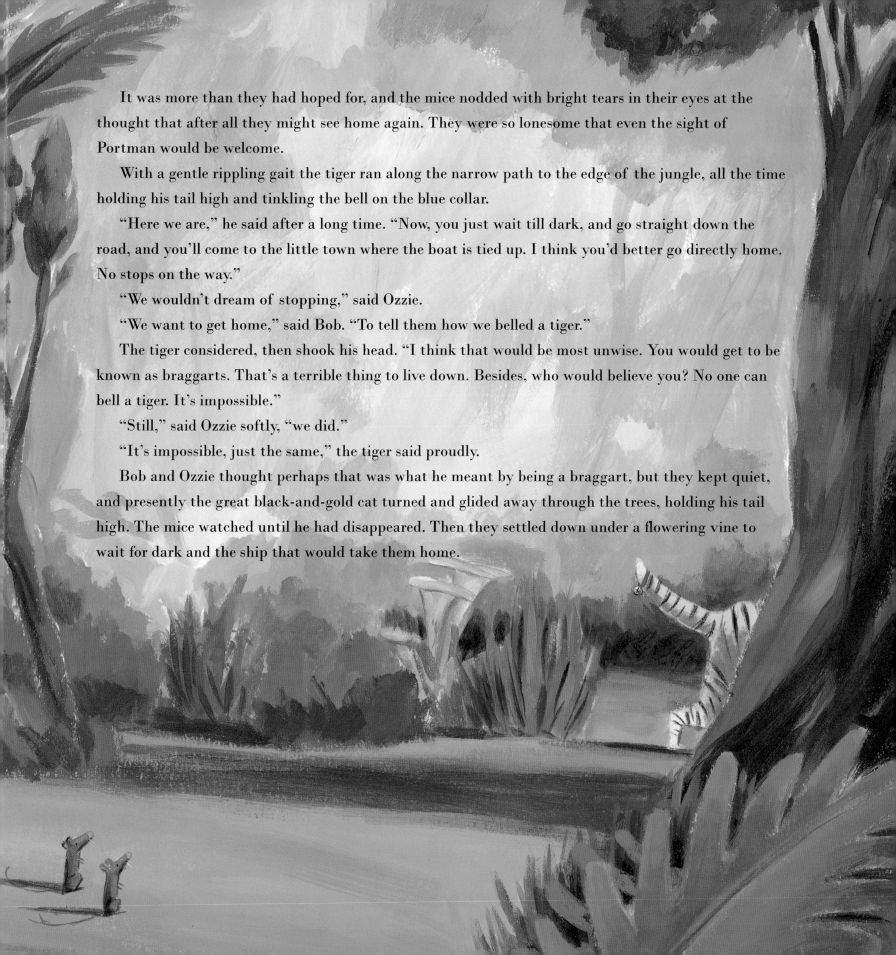

It was more than they had hoped for, and the mice nodded with bright tears in their eyes at the thought that after all they might see home again. They were so lonesome that even the sight of Portman would be welcome.

With a gentle rippling gait the tiger ran along the narrow path to the edge of the jungle, all the time holding his tail high and tinkling the bell on the blue collar.

"Here we are," he said after a long time. "Now, you just wait till dark, and go straight down the road, and you'll come to the little town where the boat is tied up. I think you'd better go directly home. No stops on the way."

"We wouldn't dream of stopping," said Ozzie.

"We want to get home," said Bob. "To tell them how we belled a tiger."

The tiger considered, then shook his head. "I think that would be most unwise. You would get to be known as braggarts. That's a terrible thing to live down. Besides, who would believe you? No one can bell a tiger. It's impossible."

"Still," said Ozzie softly, "we did."

"It's impossible, just the same," the tiger said proudly.

Bob and Ozzie thought perhaps that was what he meant by being a braggart, but they kept quiet, and presently the great black-and-gold cat turned and glided away through the trees, holding his tail high. The mice watched until he had disappeared. Then they settled down under a flowering vine to wait for dark and the ship that would take them home.

THE VOYAGE BACK was very like the trip out, except that now they had no collar to tote, so it was easier to slip down the rope and away toward town while the big dock cat washed his ears with his eyes closed.

There was a great commotion when they got back to the house. The kitchen mouse said that Portman was very angry with them for going away without permission.

"He's holding a meeting in the closet right now," said the kitchen mouse, "and I'll have to take you to him. Oh, I'm very very sorry for you, Bob and Ozzie."

"It wasn't our fault," said Bob.

"As if that mattered to Portman when he's angry," said the kitchen mouse. "Follow me, you poor things."

"Silence in the closet!" called Portman when Bob and Ozzie were standing before him. "Silence! Now"—he leaned forward, glaring, bristling, big as a badger in his outrage— "now, what have you two to say for yourselves?"

Bob and Ozzie waited to be terror-struck, as they'd always been in the old days. But the minutes passed and they simply didn't get frightened. If you're a world traveler who's belled a tiger and sent an elephant squealing into the jungle, it's difficult to be afraid of a mouse, even a mouse as angry and important as Portman.

"Well? Well?" said Portman. "Speak up! What do you say?"

Ozzie looked at Bob and then back to Portman. "We say we'd like to be moved up from the cellar," he said.

Bob nodded. "We want to be pantry mice."

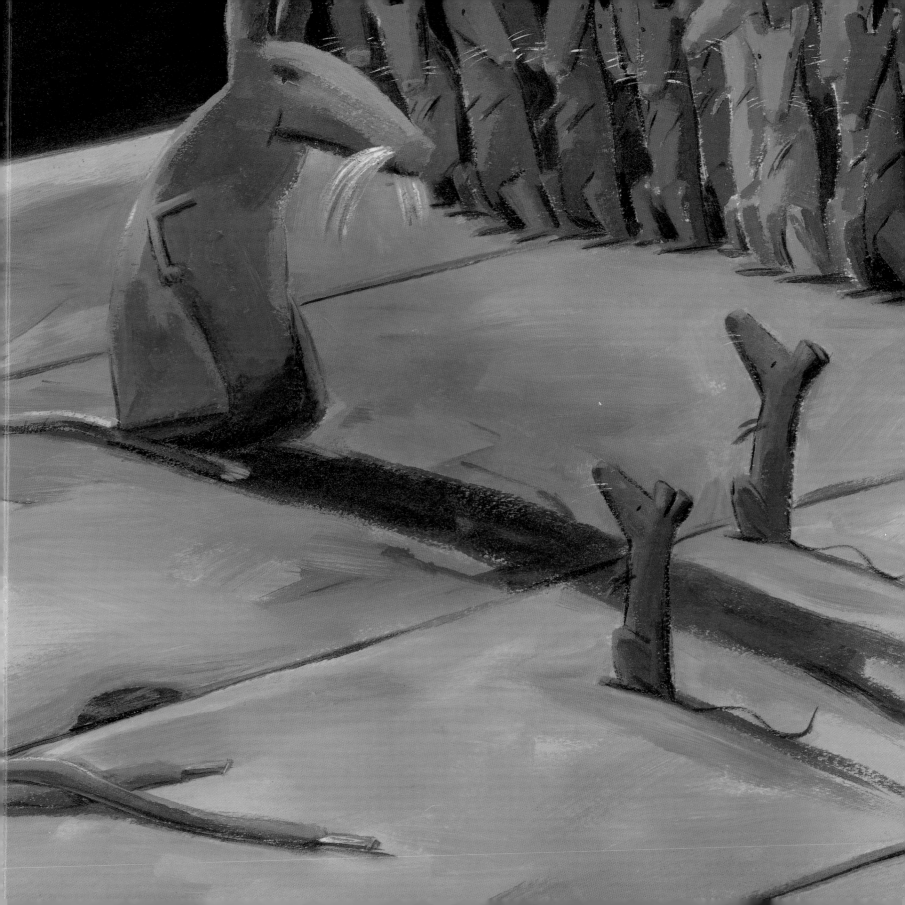

THERE WAS A RUSTLE OF ASTONISHMENT over the meeting, and Portman looked as if he were going to drop his whiskers. "What was that?" he demanded, giving them a second chance to be frightened. "I dare you to say that again!"

"We think we have enough experience now to be pantry mice," said Ozzie firmly.

Portman looked around for help and then sat down with a thud. "Humph," he said. "Humph, humph." He scratched his ear. "What makes you think that?" he said at last. "After all, you just got carried away on a boat by mistake. You act as if you'd done something brave."

Ozzie and Bob did not wish to be known as braggarts, and they knew no one would believe a word of their adventures, so they just stood their ground in silence. They heard the whispering behind them, and they watched Portman's fierce expression turn to a puzzled one. A long time passed, and then Portman stood up and said, "Let us have a show of hands. Shall these cocky mice be elevated to the pantry or not?"

"Aye, aye," shouted the mice, delighted that someone at last had stood up to the tyrannical chief mouse.

"So voted," said Portman grumpily. "See that you don't disgrace us." He allowed
a moment's applause, then lifted his paw for silence. "And now to the second matter
on our agenda. The most important news of the day is this: *It is impossible to bell a cat!*"

There was a great outcry and agitation in the closet, and Portman had to squeak his loudest to regain
their attention.

"It is true," he said when at last the meeting had come to order. "The living-room mouse and I myself
heard the father of the children read a story in which the mice did the very thing that we have done. They
met in a closet and decided to bell the cat. It seems it isn't an original idea at all . . . whoever had it."

Portman had had it, but no one pointed this out.

"According to this story," he went on, "it is customary for mice to want to bell the cat, and it is customary
for them to fail to do it. We are not here to fly in the face of custom. If the book says a cat can't be belled,
then a cat can't be belled. So let's not hear any more on the subject."

He sat down amid some boos and scattered applause.

"Just the same," said Ozzie as he and Bob curled in a corner of the pantry that night, "we did bell a very large cat. Not that anyone would believe us."

"We can believe each other," said Bob.

After a long silence Ozzie said, "I'm glad Portman doesn't know that he could scare an elephant."

"So am I," said Bob drowsily. "There'd be no living with him."

They looped their tails across each other's backs and fell asleep.